A Dragon Goes to the Dentist
My Dragon Books - Volume 57
Written by Steve Herman

Copyright © 2022 by Digital Golden Solutions LLC.
Published by DG Books Publishing, an imprint of Digital Golden Solutions LLC.

All rights reserved. No part of this publication may be reproduced, distributed, or transmitted in any form or by any means, including photocopying, recording, or other electronic or mechanical methods, without the prior written permission of the publisher, except in the case of brief quotations embodied in critical reviews and certain other noncommercial uses permitted by copyright law.

Information contained within this book is for entertainment and educational purposes only. Although the author and publisher have made every effort to ensure that the information in this book was correct at press time, the author and publisher do not assume and hereby disclaim any liability to any party for any loss, damage, or disruption caused by errors or omissions, whether such errors or omissions result from negligence, accident, or any other cause.

ISBN: 978-1-64916-130-7 (paperback)
ISBN: 978-1-64916-131-4 (hardcover)

www.MyDragonBooks.com

First Edition: June 2022
10 9 8 7 6 5 4 3 2 1

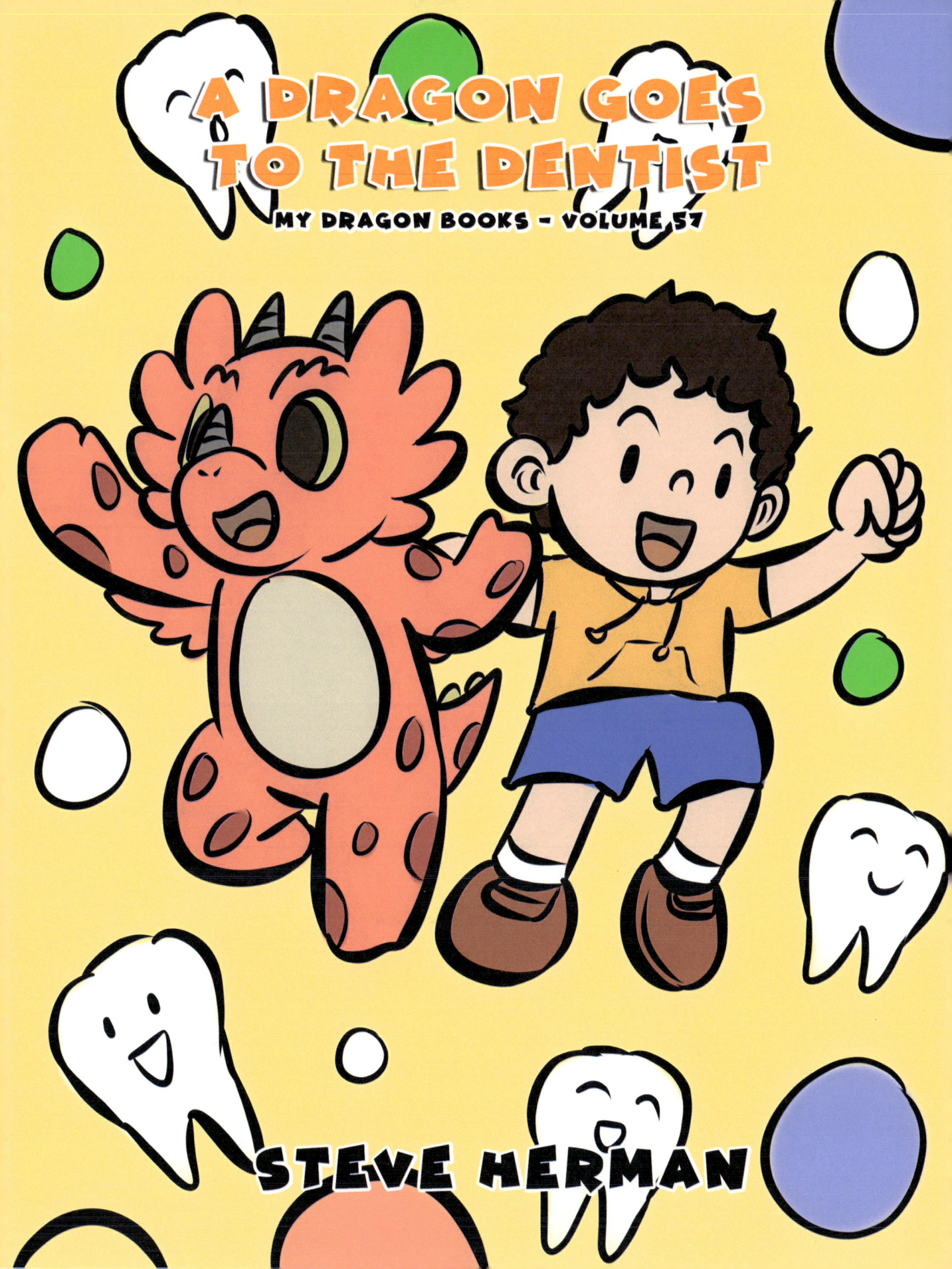

"It's time to get a check-up, Diggory," Dad said. "Let's go!"
But Diggory threw a tantrum. Yes, he put on quite a show

"I know you're scared," I told him, "but there's no need to be; I've seen the dentist LOTS of times. It's not so bad – You'll see!"

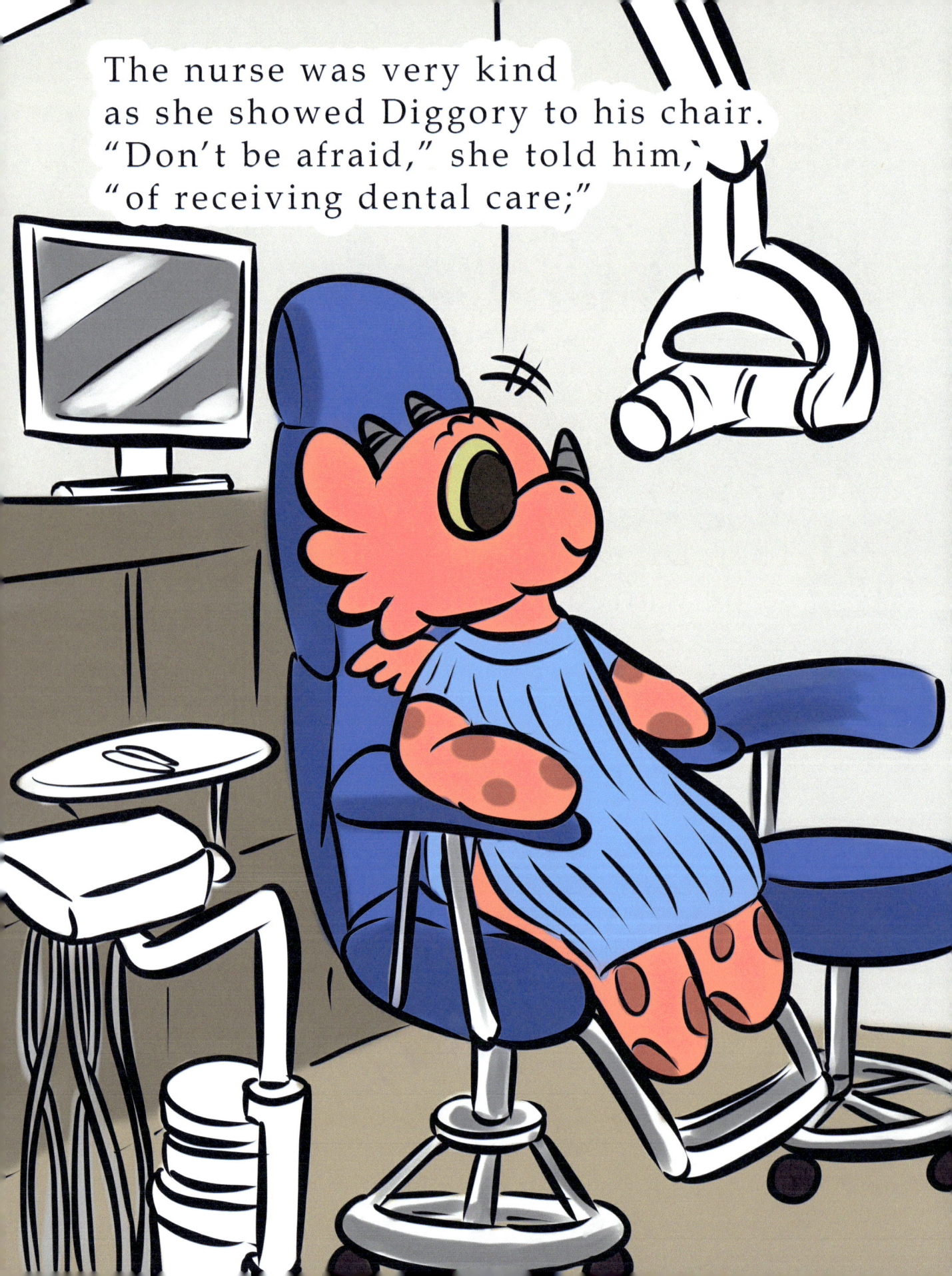

The nurse was very kind as she showed Diggory to his chair. "Don't be afraid," she told him, "of receiving dental care;"

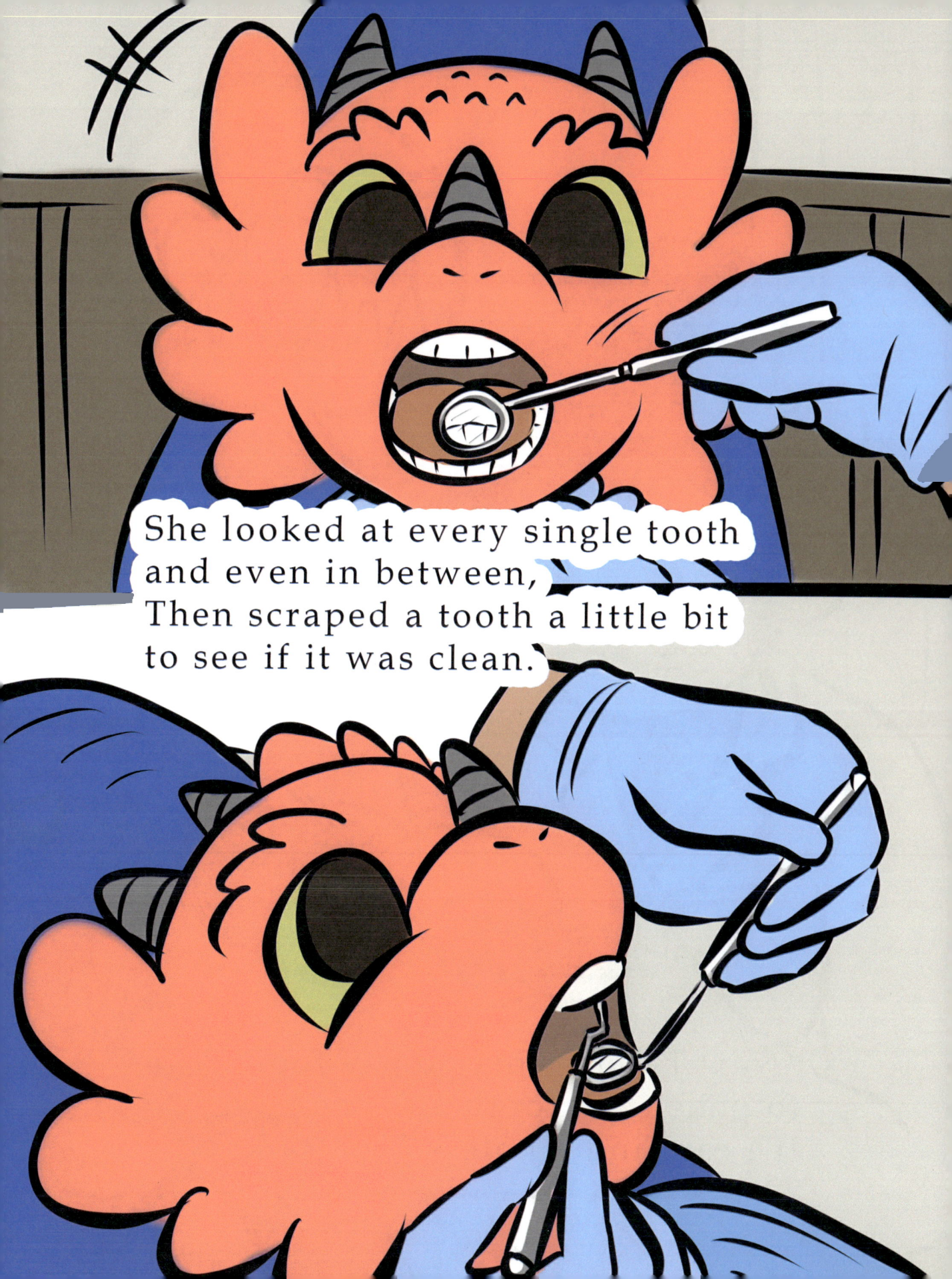

She rinsed his mouth with something sort of like a water gun,
Then used a tube that sucked it up as soon as she was done.

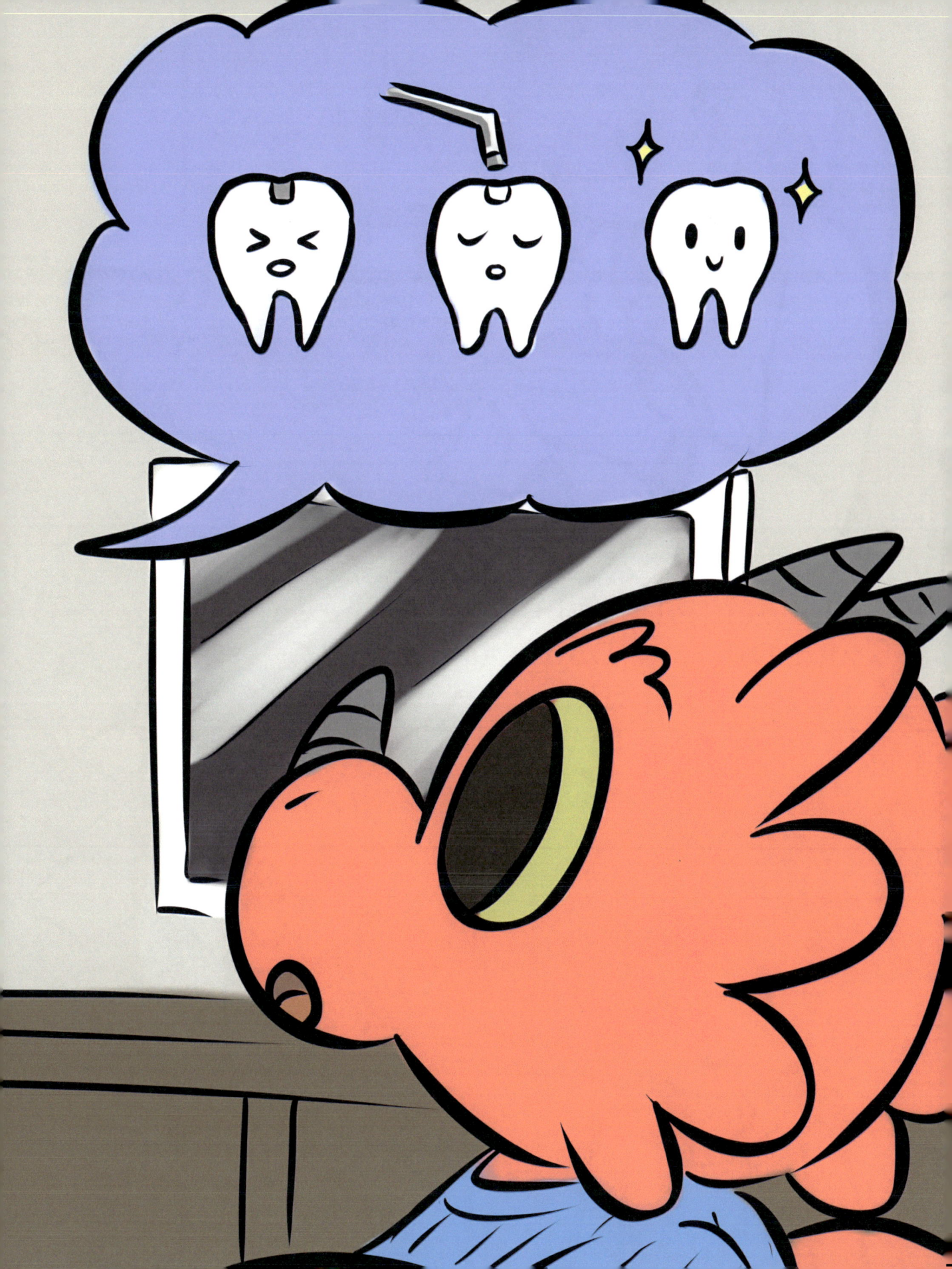

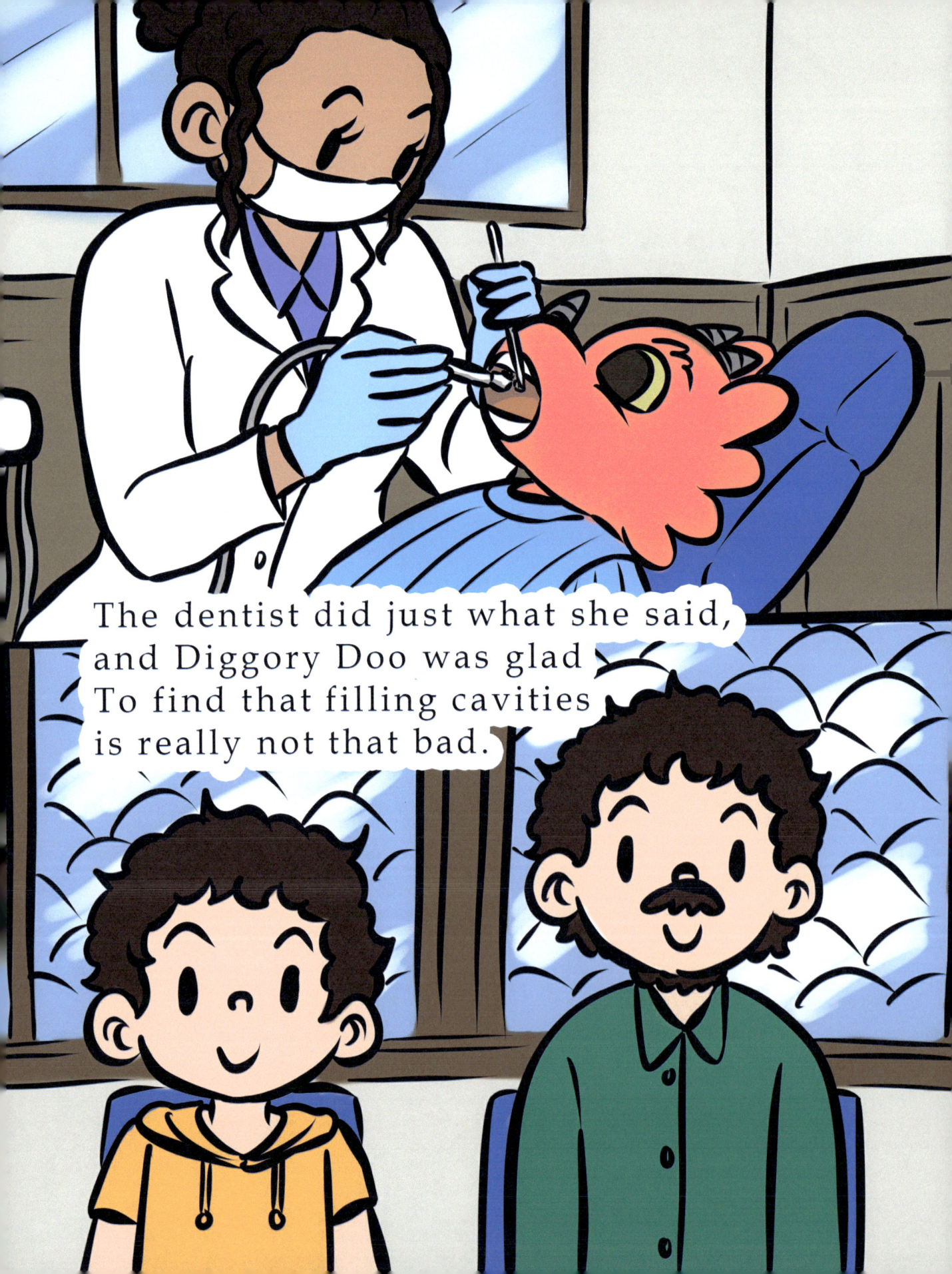

The dentist did just what she said, and Diggory Doo was glad To find that filling cavities is really not that bad.

Then Dr. Rosenthal showed Diggory Doo the proper way
That he must brush and floss his teeth at least two times a day.

That night, he brushed and flossed his teeth before he went to bed.
Then when we tucked Diggory in all warm and snug, he said,

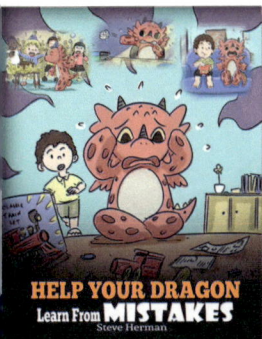

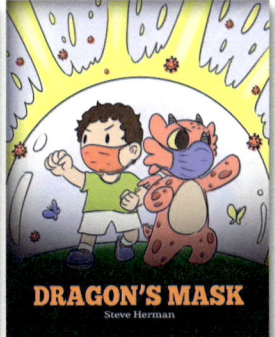

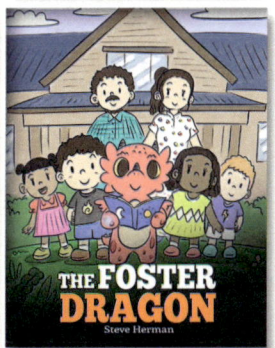
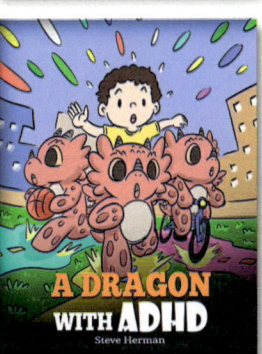

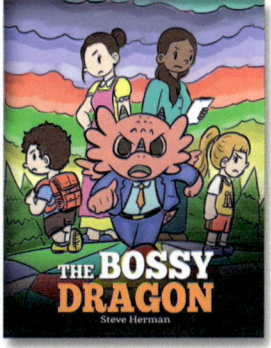

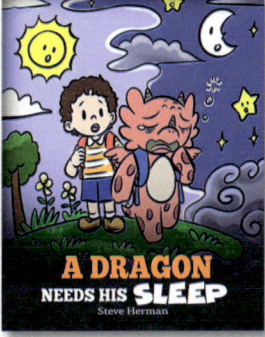

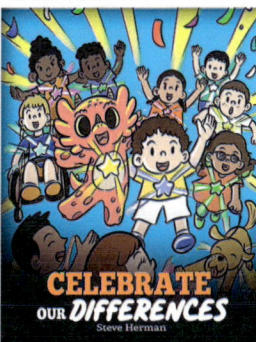

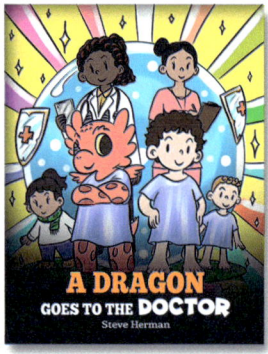

Made in the USA
Columbia, SC
18 March 2025

55330864R00027